C0-AVD-686

PUNCH: His Life and Adventures

PUNCH:
His Life
AND ADVENTURES
by Octave Feuillet

Translated from the French by Paul McPharlin
With the Original Illustrations by Bertall
and a Few Words on Making Puppets
by the Translator

A Didier Book
NEW YORK

Copyright 1946 by Didier, Publishers
Printed in the United States of America
Designed by Paul McPharlin

I

47-07252

How a Relative of the Writer Happened to Know Punch's Family—The Singular Circumstances of Our Hero's Birth—And other Incredible Matters

MY GRANDFATHER'S GREAT-UNCLE LOVED TO TRAVEL. He loved it from his childhood. Yet it turned out—though it has nothing to do with this story—that he was all of sixty before he stirred from the streets of Montmartre where he was born.

"It's just ridiculous," he often said, "that the mature person who most wants to travel is the

5

3 1172 02117 0816

one who has seen least of the world. I don't call it seeing the world to take a walk from my house in the Rue St. Denis to the windmills out on the outskirts of Montmartre. I'm really an ass—that's the daily route of asses with loads of grain."

By dint of such brooding my grandfather's great-uncle one fine morning eventually worked himself to the point of taking the stagecoach for Marseilles. There he sailed for Naples. He had planned to go to the Orient, the Indies, and the

Americas; he wanted to see them all before re-
turning to the Rue St. Denis by way of the Cape
of Good Hope. But this pretty project was nipped
in the bud. An accident befell him. He had not
been in Naples three days when he suddenly died.

This is all the more regrettable, for not only
did it cut short my grandfather's great-uncle's
trip, but it put an end to his scheme of keeping
a day-by-day account of it. Among his papers,
which were sent back to France wrapped in his
spare shirt, there is the beginning of a diary which
I am sorry could not be finished. Here is the
part which has a direct bearing on this story:

"First day. Arrived in Naples. Me-oh-my!

"Second day. My-oh-me!

"Third day. Went around the Bay with a boatman named Pulci, whose wife has just had a
singular infant that people come miles to see."

This singular infant was our hero himself, the
illustrious Pulcinello, whose Italian name children affectionately changed to Punch so that it
would be easier to say.

The boatman Pulci lived with his wife in a little
white house near the shore where he moored his
boat. They had been married twenty years and
grieved because they had no children. It was
particularly hard on poor Dame Pulci, who was

left alone a great part of the time while her husband was fishing or taking out sightseers.

In her loneliness the good woman had bought a little cradle, for want of something better, to comfort her aching heart. Sometimes she would

sit by herself singing a sweet, monotonous folk-song beside the empty basket as if she were lulling a baby to sleep.

One evening when Dame Pulci was complaining as usual that Heaven refused her the baby she so much wanted, old Pulci, disliking his wife to go on so about it—besides, he had been drinking—jumped up, banged the table with his fist, and cried, "Devil quiet this grumbler!"

"Holy Virgin," said Dame Pulci quickly, "have pity on us!"

No sooner had she uttered these words than a big cat, black as soot, came out as if from under the bed, jumped against the legs of the worthy Pulci, threw him over on the floor, and escaped through the half-open door. At the same time a little bird, hidden in a fold of the heavy curtains, flew out across the room, gently pecked the hair of Dame Pulci as it passed her, and disappeared through the window.

Before the couple could recover from their first fright another strange thing happened to terrify them. From the cradle came a cry so peculiar and unusual that it sounded as if someone had a peach stone stuck in his throat.

"Wife, see what that is," said the trembling Pulci, who was still lying where he had been thrown by the big cat.

All excited, the poor woman went over to the cradle. She almost died of joy; in it she saw a tiny human creature, wriggling and thumping its arms against its belly in great good spirits.

"By all the saints, what a pretty baby!" exclaimed Dame Pulci, snatching it up in her arms. A mother's eyes are indulgent; they can find no fault with a hump more or less. Of course this pretty baby had only two, one on his stomach like a comma, the other on his back, by way of

counterbalance, like an exclamation point. As for his face, there was nothing so unpleasant about it, save perhaps the nose, which was rather like a parrot's beak, curving down to meet a hooked chin, so that the two made a kind of porch for the large door of a mouth.

"Pretty baby! Sweet treasure!" cried the good woman over and over, fondling it tenderly.

"Let me have a look at it," said father Pulci. In his growing amazement, he lay obstinately

where the cat had thrown him. "Let's see it." But when he had seen it he roared, "What an ugly brat! A fine son, with two humps! Isn't he ashamed to have a nose like that? Give him to me and I'll throw him into the sea."

But that isn't what happened. Upon father Pulci's words the little fellow jumped out of his mother's arms. You should have seen him caper on his spindly legs and go through such contortions and make such faces that you would have split your sides laughing. Then suddenly he balanced himself on his front hump, spun like a top

and fell at the knees of father Pulci, making the
funniest grimace you ever saw and taking him
gently by the beard. Father Pulci, who had never
laughed so much in all his life and who had

cramps from it for a week after, could resist no
longer and hugged the child affectionately.

"That settles it," he said to his overjoyed wife.
"Whether he comes from the devil or not, or has
a hump or not, I'll keep him—he's so funny."

"Pulci," she replied, "I'm sure that the big black
cat was the devil—or a close relative—and that
the little bird came from the good Lord."

"Wife, you are right," agreed the good fellow.
"I can see that both of them had something to
do with Punch's birth. For I admit that if he's
ugly as the devil he has the spirit of an angel."

II

Remarkable Progress of Young Punch—How He Curried Favor at Court—The Adventure of the Tight-Rope-Walking Donkey—How Punch Got Rid of a Blackamoor Ambassador

AFTER SIX WEEKS PUNCH HAD GROWN SO FAST AND his wits had matured so far beyond his age, that you would have taken him to be at least sixteen. He had a glib tongue and a sharp mind and often embarrassed his parents by asking questions which they could not answer. Seeing that he was so big, his father decided to make a porter of him, for nice as he was, he felt that he could not be permitted to become a burden. By good luck

14

he had grown up fast, so advantage had to be taken of it.

One morning at breakfast Pulci therefore said, "Well, Punch, you're a big boy now and can earn your own living. I suggest that you go down to the harbor and find something to do running errands and carrying baggage for travellers."

"Hm," said Punch politely, "I've a better idea."

"What's that?" asked his father.

"I'll go to court."

"Imagine!" cried the good man, with peals of laughter, "to court! And what would you do there, you little monkey? You don't expect me to introduce you! I've no connections there."

"Then I'll introduce myself!"

15

"And what makes you think you want to go to court?"

"I'll tell you. Since I've a hump fore and aft, I'd better learn to read and write. The Lord willing, I'll become a scholar. I'll be so brilliant that nobody will notice my humps or my looks. You are too poor to give me an education, so the king might as well do it. I feel pretty sure that I can persuade him to. But first I'll need a donkey."

"A donkey!" exclaimed both father and mother Pulci. "Where could we get you a donkey? Punch, child, don't you know that donkeys don't grow on horse-chestnut trees?"

"Well, why not sell your little house? I promise you a bigger one, all furnished in the latest style. With the money you get you can buy me a donkey right away."

"Wife, this boy of yours is crazy!" growled Pulci. "Devil take him and his donkey!"

"It's you, sir, that's crazy," retorted the good woman. "Don't you see that the child has a lot more imagination than you ever had?"

To make a long story short, after a good hour of arguing, Pulci permitted himself to be won over by one of Punch's funny capers; he sold his house that very afternoon, bought the donkey, and waited to see what would happen.

When he got his donkey Punch mounted it as if he had ridden all his life, and where do you suppose he went? Straight to the king's palace. His father and mother followed him a distance behind, for, having sold their house, they had nowhere else to go. A crowd fell in behind him, shouting in glee; he made quite a spectacle with his two glistening humps, his skin-tight costume, half red and half yellow, his flame-colored shoes, and his tall gilt hat, as he rode along on his donkey, as solemn as could be. When he drew near the palace he was being followed by more than three thousand people, not counting the cats, dogs, and butterflies.

The king, hearing the hubbub, stepped out on his balcony, and all the court crowded to the windows, curious to know what the strange little humpback wanted. Silence fell when Punch gave three bows to the king and the royal family, and then held up his hand as a sign that he wished to speak.

"Listen, listen!" cried everybody.

"Sire, ladies, gentlemen, and all you people of Naples," began Punch in his piercing voice, "I have the honor to announce that, with the permission of His Majesty, my donkey will dance on the tight-rope before this distinguished assemblage. The rope will be stretched fifty-one feet from the ground. Your servant, Punch, will ride the donkey as he performs this amazing feat of equilibrium."

"Hear, hear!" cried the delighted crowd, applauding. "Hurrah for Punch! Hurrah for the donkey! Hurrah for the king!"

Having bowed acknowledgment for this acclaim, the king called down, "When do you start? I declare that I'd like very much to see this feat."

"Sire, this evening at seven," replied Punch, "if Your Majesty will have his majordomo provide me with what I need—rope, poles, ladder, and all that."

"Most certainly," said the king. "Let my majordomo approach."

It must be explained that this majordomo, whose name was Lord Boogoo-Roogoo, was a wicked person, hated everywhere in the realm for his black heart and cruel sport. For instance, a while before this, he had ordered Punch's father to be beaten almost to death on the ridiculous charge that the poor old man had stepped on the foot of one of his lordship's horses.

"Lord Boogoo-Roogoo," said the king, "I charge you to provide this interesting hunchback with

whatever may be necessary. If by your negligence we are deprived of our evening's diversion, I'll straightway hang you. But if Punch is boasting of something he cannot do, it is he who will hang."

"Sire, it's agreed," said Punch.

"Let food be given to him and the donkey," commanded the king.

Thereupon Punch was taken into one of the courtyards of the palace and given excellent leavings from the royal table, of which you may be sure his father and mother had the best part. These poor people were not at all easy about the outcome of the adventure, for it was difficult for them to see how Punch could manage to get his donkey to dance on a tightrope fifty feet in the air. They could already envision their dear little hunchback dangling with a rope around his neck and the king jeering at him.

"Don't be so downcast," said Punch. "Eat your fill and leave it to me to manage."

Evening fell. By order of the majordomo two poles fifty-one feet tall had been erected in the square facing the palace and a rope stretched between them. Three magnificent pavilions of gold-brocade tapestry, decked out with pennants in the royal colors, had been hastily erected. The whole court had taken seats in the rich stands, and the king was on his throne in the middle pavilion. The people jammed the square. They perched on tables, chairs, carts, roofs, and on each other's backs. Then a great shout went up, "There he is! There he is!"

Punch entered riding on his donkey and doffing his gilt hat to left and right. Lord Boogoo-Roogoo, who had remained in the square to see that nothing was lacking for the ceremonies, held Punch's stirrup as he got down from his mount. A ladder had been placed against one of the poles from which the rope was stretched. Punch lightly ran up and was at the top in no time; he continued to wave his hat.

"Hurray," yelled the crowd, "watch, the donkey is going to dance." "Really?" "On all four feet?" "Will he need a balancing pole?"

Meanwhile Lord Boogoo-Roogoo was holding the donkey by the bridle at the foot of the ladder.

"Go ahead, Punch," cried the king. "That's enough bowing. Start your performance. I'm waiting to see it."

"Sire," replied Punch from the top of the ladder, "I'm ready."

After waiting a moment and seeing that Punch did not move, the king repeated angrily, "All right, go ahead. What's keeping you?"

"With all respect, Sire," said Punch humbly, "I'm waiting for the donkey."

"The donkey?" replied the king hotly. "Don't make fun of me! Didn't you promise to have it dance on the tightrope?"

"Sire, I still promise," said Punch, "but he must be up here. While I can make him dance on the tightrope to perfection, I haven't the slightest idea of how to make him climb the ladder. I'll make him dance; your majordomo has to get him up. I was told that I'd have everything necessary. It's the donkey that I need most!"

At these words the whole court burst out laughing. The people applauded. No one was sorry to see Lord Boogoo-Roogoo so embarrassed. The king himself rolled on his throne in laughter, and had to wipe his eyes several times before he could find his voice.

"Do you hear, Lord Boogoo-Roogoo?" said the king at last. "I warn you to comply with the just demand of Punch."

"But, Sire—" protested Lord Boogoo-Roogoo, bursting with rage.

"No explanations," interrupted the king. "Get the donkey up."

Then Lord Boogoo-Roogoo, dragging the donkey to the foot of the ladder, tried to persuade it

to climb. It refused to understand. "Giddap, gid-dap!" urged Lord Boogoo-Roogoo.

"Hee haw! Hee haw!" brayed the donkey, to the delight of the crowd.

"You miserable beast," repeated the major-domo, "giddap!"

"Hee haw! Hee haw!" repeated the animal, obstinately bracing itself on its front legs.

"You villain, you!" rejoined the majordomo, pushing the donkey from behind with such violent efforts that he went purple.

"Hee haw! Hee haw!"

"There, take that!" cried Lord Boogoo-Roogoo, raining kicks on it. The donkey, which by now had a natural grievance, let fly with its hind legs

and sprawled the majordomo on the pavement.

"Hurrah! Hurrah!" cried the people, and the court went into transports of joy.

Meanwhile Punch had got down from the ladder. He picked up Lord Boogoo-Roogoo, who had not been hurt, though he pretended to be as an excuse to run away into the depths of the palace. In a bound Punch was before the royal pavilion and on his knees, asking pardon with such a funny air of being sorry that the king said, "Indeed, you little imp, I grant your pardon, but on this condition: that you set your unusual imagination to work and get me out of the terrible fix about my daughter's marriage."

This is the kind of a fix it was: everybody in Naples knew about it. Some years before, the king's capital city had been in danger from the Turkish fleet and he had asked the Blackamoor

king for help in soldiers and money. The Blackamoor king had come to his aid, stipulating that
as a reward he was to receive the princess of
Naples in marriage when she was old enough. She
was known throughout the world for her remarkable beauty. The king of Naples was in no position to refuse this bargain and had to agree to it.
The Turks thereupon were cut to pieces by the
combined troops of the two sovereigns.

Since then the princess had grown up, and on
the very day when Punch made his bow at court,
the ambassador of the Blackamoor king had arrived in great pomp with five hundred little Blackamoors in his suite, all wearing tiger skins and

golden bands on their arms, legs, and necks. The ambassador had come to claim the princess for his master. Everybody deplored so unsuitable a match, for the princess was as lovely of face and as pleasant of character as the Blackamoor king was ugly and ill-natured.

So the crowd set up a murmur of approval when Punch replied, "Sire, it would be a pity to send the princess, a star of beauty, to live among the lions, tigers, and Blackamoors."

"My very thought," said the king, while the princess furtively wiped a sparkling tear from the corner of her lovely eye. "But what am I to do? I've given my word; it's a debt of honor."

"Didn't the bargain concern you both?" asked Punch. "Wasn't the Blackamoor king somehow obligated too?"

"Alas," said the king, "I was in such straits with the Turks so near that I had to promise anything he wanted—and he wanted my daughter. As a gesture of triumph, my son-in-law-to-be added a flippant clause to the bargain, saying that he would give the princess a wedding present of a pair of slippers made of as costly a material as she might wish, providing it was to be found on the face of the earth."

"Why, then," cried Punch, "dry your tears, princess! The Blackamoor king won't touch so much as the tip of your little finger. Sire, allow me to speak to the ambassador. I'll send him home to blackamoor with his Blackamoors."

Shaking his head with an air of doubt, the king summoned the ambassador of the Blackamoor king, who with his retinue occupied the pavilion to the left. When he came into the royal presence, everyone listened in a hush while Punch addressed him. "Sir," said he, "I see that you are an intelligent man. You would not wish to take this princess away against her will."

"It is my order and I shall take her," said he bluntly.

"So," said Punch. "But, sir, it would be very little trouble for you to make the king and his daughter happy without displeasing your master. You could tell him, for instance, that she has grown suddenly so ugly that she'd curdle milk, or that she's gone crazy, or taken to stammering, or become club-footed, or sprouted a couple of humps like mine, or anything else to make him lose his interest in her."

"What nonsense! No, thanks, my fine friend. Away with you and your humps!" said the ambassador.

"So that's your tune?" replied Punch. "Then I can play it too. Sir, are you not obligated by your bargain to give the princess a gift of a pair of slippers such as she may desire?"

"To be sure," sniffed the ambassador. "And they can be made of anything under the sun."

"Excellent. And if you refuse to give them, the marriage is off?"

"Naturally," said the ambassador, smiling insolently.

"Well, then, sir, the princess, who has the best of taste, knows nothing under the sun that has such a nice shiny black as your skin, so please make her a pair of slippers of it, with good thick soles, and let's have no further delay. However, if you prefer to keep your skin for your personal use, tell your master whatever you want, but don't bother us in the future. Good-bye, sir; go get yourself skinned."

The ambassador, who probably had reasons for wanting to wear his skin, made no other reply but to take to his heels, followed by the five hundred little Blackamoors. Not stopping even to pay their debts, they embarked and sailed away. But the king of Naples was so overjoyed that he proclaimed he would settle their bills for them so that no one might be worried in this happy hour.

Meanwhile Punch was showered with polite attentions from the courtiers, who were not unaware that he was now in favor. In fact, the king lost no time in asking him what he would like for the good turn he had done the royal family.

"Sire," said Punch, "may I ask four favors of Your Majesty? First, that you take me as one of your pages and give me a liberal education."

"Let it be," said the king.

"Second, that my donkey, to which I am so indebted, may be retired from carrying grain to the mill, to browse on your royal lawn."

"Let it browse," said the king.

"Third, that my parents may live in comfort to the end of their days."

"Let them so live," said the king. "And fourth?"

"That I may have the hand of the princess—to kiss."

The king assented, the princess with a warm smile graciously extended her hand, and, while the crowd went wild at his display of good manners, Punch gently kissed her four fingers, but stopped at her thumb.

III

Punch as Page to the King—The Three Mishaps of Lord Boogoo-Roogoo—The First Mishap—Punch's Secret

THAT VERY EVENING PUNCH WAS TAKEN INTO THE king's palace as a page. His father and mother were not forgotten, but given a pretty cottage in the royal park in a grove of orange trees. Dame Pulci had nothing to do but spin thread of gold and silk for the princess, who often came by on her morning walk to chat with the good couple.

Punch's fellow pages were at first tempted to tease him because of his deformity and ugliness, but soon they all became his friends, some dreading the barb of his famous wit, others liking his unfailing good nature, for when wit is united with kindness, the resulting amiability of character wins the world, and a comely face is the last thing by which sensible people judge one.

BAULANT

According to his wish, Punch had teachers in every liberal subject. He knew that intelligence

is useless without learning and determined to
study until his accomplishments might outweigh
his humps and outshine his face. It has been seen
how his play of imagination lifted him to ac-
quaintance with the king and the gratitude of the
princess. From that evening of their first meeting,
she never passed him without giving him something nice, like lemon drops or licorice sticks or
peppermint candy, of which he was very fond.

But Punch was not destined to enjoy his good
fortune in peace. He had made a powerful enemy

in Lord Ernest Boogoo-Roogoo, who had not for-
given him for having made him a laughing-stock
before the court. Lord Boogoo-Roogoo, as grand

majordomo, had charge of the pages' quarters and lost no opportunity to discredit the poor two-humped page before the king. If a practical joke was played, if, for instance, a courtier found a mouse eating nuts in his pocket, or an ambassador paced into the solemn audience chamber trailing a little paper cart from his train, "That's Punch again!" said Lord Boogoo-Roogoo. "You can see his work." But the king paid no attention, until the majordomo lost all patience and made up his mind to stop at nothing in order to achieve his end.

He knew that the king had taken a particular liking to a little fire-red bird which had been sent him by the sultan of Bengal. This little bird was silent during the day, but as twilight fell it sang so beautifully that it brought tears to the eyes of anyone so fortunate as to hear it.

Lord Boogoo-Roogoo, like all insensitive and wicked people, disliked music. He wrung the neck of the little bird and hid its body under Punch's bed. The next day when all the palace was thunderstruck at the disappearance of the favorite bird, Lord Boogoo-Roogoo had the pages' quarters searched, and there, naturally, the blood-red little thing was found where he had put it. The king was beside himself. Without even listening to Punch, he ordered that his majordomo forthwith give him fifty lashes, in the usual place.

Punch felt this indignity very keenly and did not accept the injustice without harboring a violent grudge against Lord Ernest. Having observed that the majordomo was careful of his appearance to the point of foppishness, and that he thought himself the handsomest man in the world, Punch resolved to attack him at this point.

The next day every nook of the palace was plastered with little notices, written by hand, which said, "To appear shortly, 73½ ways to tie a cravat, by Lord B * *-R * *." The court did not lose the chance to amuse itself at the expense of the grand majordomo, who was far from doubtful about the source of this mortification.

Another time at a royal ball this wicked nobleman, who was vain of his lightness in dancing, suddenly found himself, just as he was about to execute a leap, unable to raise a foot; the soles of his shoes had secretly been covered with tar which, when it warmed, stuck fast to the floor. It took four strong footmen to pull him away. He had broken out in perspiration during his struggle and humiliation, and wiped his face without noticing that his handkerchief was filled with soot. He went at once to a mirror, and you may be sure he was the only one who did not think his black mask funny.

Some time after this unhappy adventure the court was discussing Lord Boogoo-Roogoo's rich costumes. "You wouldn't think it," said Punch, who happened to be there, "but they serve as a covering for—"

"For what?" asked the king.

"Why, Your Majesty doesn't know?"

"Know what?"

"Sire, the first courtier you meet can tell you."

So the king asked his courtiers, but they all said they had no idea what Punch meant.

Devoured by curiosity, the king returned to his page and urged him to explain.

"Sire," said Punch, "I thought it was public knowledge. But since I alone seem to know, it seems that discretion should seal my lips."

"Take me into the secret; it is my royal command!"

Whispering into the king's ear, Punch said, "Lord Ernest Boogoo-Roogoo has feathers."

"What!" exclaimed the king, "feathers! Can it be possible!"

"All over."

"Ha!" cried the king, "no wonder he dances so lightly! Feathers! It's wonderful!"

"They cover his body so that it's hard for him to sit down."

At this the king burst out laughing and rubbed his hands in glee.

The lords and ladies present, seeing the king laugh and suspecting that the page's secret was a good one, drew him aside, each begging to be

taken into his confidence. "All right," said Punch
to them one by one, "I'll tell you if you keep it
to yourself." Then he repeated what he had told
the king. Because he told the story confidentially
to everybody, as a secret to be kept, there was
soon nobody in the palace down to the last scul-
lion, who didn't know that Lord Boogoo-Roogoo
had feathers under his clothes. That's why a secret
that isn't a secret is called Punch's secret.

Now the gentleman under discussion came to
the royal card tables. There were chuckles, winks,
and smiles, the cause of which he hadn't the
slightest idea. Some people even tiptoed up to
peep into his collar to see where the plumage
began. The worst of it was that Lord Boogoo-
Roogoo, having lost several games, happened to

drop the remark to the king, "Sire, I've been plucked!"

At this the court choked with laughter and the king couldn't resist replying, "Indeed, my dear Ernest, you deserved it."

Lord Boogoo-Roogoo could not imagine what in the world it was that prompted all these smiles and odd replies, and left in embarrassment to puzzle over what had happened.

Punch did not, however, consider his account settled with so little as this. He had noticed that the grand majordomo stole off at the same time every evening to a summerhouse deep in the garden, where he dug in a certain spot. Curious to know what it was all about, Punch dug in the same place and found a bag of gold pieces. Lord Ernest was a miser, and for fear of being robbed (the wicked are always suspicious) he had buried his money. Punch was far too honest to be tempted to take what belonged to another, so he carefully replaced the sod over his discovery, and ran capering back to the king, who was supping in his great marble hall.

"What's up?" asked the king, seeing him.

"Sire," said Punch in a low voice, "your grand majordomo is getting to be so much like a bird that he not only has feathers but lays eggs!"

"What!" exclaimed his majesty. "Ernest! Eggs!"

"I'm sure of it," replied Punch.

"Humpf!" said the king.

"Sire, if Your Majesty wishes to come with me tomorrow evening," responded the prankish page, "all his doubts will be laid at rest."

The next evening the king and Punch crept stealthily through the palace gardens, the king curious to see his grand majordomo lay an egg, Punch delighted at the success of his ruse. When they reached the summerhouse they concealed themselves in the shrubbery. Soon after they saw

Lord Ernest go cautiously into the shelter, looking uneasily from side to side, then turn his back and crouch.

"Heavens!" said the king to Punch in a whisper, "I believe you're right. He's going to lay an egg. That's a singular notion. A man must be pretty idle to amuse himself laying eggs. But why on earth is he digging?"

"He's covering up his clutch," said Punch.

"That's that!" gasped the king, punching himself in the thigh, "you must be right. He really lays eggs."

At this point, Lord Boogoo-Roogoo having satisfied himself that his treasure was still there, went off dreaming of gold pieces.

The king took advantage of his departure to enter the summerhouse and dig in his turn. Punch lit a lantern. "Here!" pointed the king. "Right!"

said Punch, putting his knife to use and deftly slicing the earth, but not exactly in the place where he knew the treasure to be hidden.

"Why, here's an egg!" exclaimed the king, who was watching the operation with the closest attention. "Two! Three! Four!" He kept on counting until a dozen had been uncovered. "By my royal crown," cried he, touching them gingerly, "you'd think they were turkey eggs!"

The exalted monarch was not mistaken, for Punch had taken them that very morning from the poultry yard.

"Our mind is made up," declared the king. "We shall take them, for we know what we're going to do with them." He gathered them up into a corner of his robe and returned to the palace, Punch leading the way with the lantern.

Now there was an academy of a dozen learned men at Naples whose duty it was to investigate all phenomena of science and the arts. That same night the king called this illustrious company together, told it of the singular fact which Punch had disclosed, and taking the twelve eggs from his lap, passed them around.

An investigation started. A stove was brought and one egg was soft boiled. Others were made into an omelette and three of the academicians who were most zealous in the pursuit of science were charged with tasting it. Upon the report of these learned men the academy, speaking through its president, rendered the following important decision: "The eggs of Lord Boogoo-Roogoo, though like turkey eggs in size and shape, are completely different in flavor, having something of a pineapple taste about them. This extraordinary fact deserves further investigation. Lord Boogoo-Roogoo should be asked, in the name of the king and in the interest of science, to lay forthwith a special clutch which, divided into several parts, may be sent to foreign academies for study."

Despite the lateness of the hour, a delegation of academicians went to inform Lord Boogoo-Roogoo of this decision. He had gone to bed. No sooner did he receive the message than he jumped

up in a fury, waving his arms so freely about that the savants could no longer be deluded that he was covered with feathers, or that the eggs were anything but another invention of Punch.

It has never been decided who was more covered with confusion, the academicians or Lord Ernest. But of this there was no doubt, that all swore to take revenge upon Punch for the silly part he had caused them to play.

IV

*The Second Mishap of Lord Boogoo-Roogoo—
What Happened to this Nobleman's Periwig and
to Those of the Academicians*

THE NEXT DAY LORD BOOGOO-ROOGOO, FOLLOWED
by the twelve academicians, came for an audience
with the king. For all his dignity the monarch
could not help a concealed smile to see them
come in. Speaking for the group, the grand majordomo addressed His Majesty with the words, "It
can only end in disaster to the nation if the affron-
teries of this whippersnapper Punch are not prop-
erly punished! Nothing is sacred to the hunchback.
He has already managed to make laughing-stocks,
not only before the court but before the whole

town, of the respectable body of the academy of sciences and of me, the grand majordomo. If he is not punished he may even take it upon himself to assault the king's own person. In brief, we humbly beseech Your Majesty to mete out justice to this terrible criminal, so that our national institutions and crown may be saved from destruction!"

Having reflected upon this discourse, the king put on a serious air and summoned Punch to his side. "My friend," said he, "I must admit that I did not fail to enjoy your last practical joke. The queen and I were awake half the night laughing about it. Nevertheless we were all your dupes, I and these gentlemen alike. It is contrary to order and a regrettable precedent. I have no alternative, I am sorry to say, but to order that you receive five hundred whacks with a stick on the soles of your feet."

"Sire," asked Punch, "may I be given the choice of the kind of stick?"

"Granted," replied the king.

"Then I'd like a peppermint stick; at least the pieces will be nice."

"I am in no mood for joking," rejoined the king seriously. "My daughter the princess has lately fallen into such a fit of melancholy that the doctors give little hope for her life unless something is found to make her laugh."

"I'll find it!" volunteered Punch. "I promise."

"You think you can make her laugh?"

"I'll do it today, sire."

"On that condition I'll let you off from the five hundred whacks. But if you fail you are to receive a thousand! Gentlemen," added the king, speaking to Lord Boogoo-Roogoo and the academicians, "you shall be the judges."

"Good enough," muttered Punch.

When the king asked Punch if he needed anything to help him carry out his promise, Punch asked for nothing but about fifteen pigeons from the royal aviary. These were granted him, and the court straightway repaired to the garden. The princess came to a window of the palace at her father's order, though she had no desire to be entertained. It was pitiful to see how pale and thin she had become, with her eyes forever wet with tears because of her sad malady.

"Dear me," said everyone, "the fear of receiving those whacks must have cracked poor Punch, if he thinks he can cure the princess with pigeons."

Especially did the group of academicians and Lord Boogoo-Roogoo cruelly taunt the hunchbacked page for his hopeless attempt.

Presently Punch made his appearance, carrying a big cage in which the king's fifteen pigeons were fluttering.

"What is he up to?" asked his majesty. "Alas, my daughter is far from amused. Frankly, I can see no reason why she should laugh at this."

Meanwhile Punch set down the cage before

Lord Boogoo-Roogoo and the academicians, cour-
teously explaining, "Gentlemen, you may thus be
in the front lines to judge the effect of my humor."

He took one of the pigeons from the cage and
held it in his hand, stroking it a moment or two
while everybody watched.

The lovely Princess continued to weep.

Suddenly Punch released the pigeon. It soared
in flight. Nobody noticed that Punch held a thread
which was attached to its foot. While Lord Boogoo-Roogoo and everybody else was watching the
flight of the bird, the sly page slipped a fishhook
tied to the pigeon's thread into the grand majordomo's periwig. Instantly the periwig followed in
flight. At this unexpected sight, such a roar of
laughter arose—what with Lord Ernest making

unheard-of high jumps in a vain attempt to recover his wig—that it could be heard three leagues
out at sea. But that was nothing when Punch,
taking advantage of the moment while everybody
stood dumbfounded, hooked the dozen periwigs
of the academicians and sent them off as trophies
with the rest of the pigeons. The lovely princess,
sober till now, went off into gales of laughter like
everybody else. In fact, they had to hold her
bodily and shake her, for she could not stop. The

king, beside himself with joy, grabbed the first person he saw, a passing baker's boy, and publicly embraced him.

The pigeons and periwigs finally disappeared into the clouds and the grand majordomo and twelve academicians with their bare pates had to make for home, amid the jeers of the Neapolitan rabble.

V

The Third and Last Mishap of Lord Ernest Boogoo-Roogoo—His Sniffles and their Singular Result

BAULANT

As a consequence all the learned men and bigwigs of the realm, taking the matter of Lord Ernest's periwig as a personal insult, marched four by four to the palace, with faces even longer than usual, to demand the death of Punch.

Having heard their request, the king replied, "Gentlemen, you are very pleasant, wishing to bring about the death of the one who has just saved the life of the princess! I should think that

Lord Boogoo-Roogoo and the members of the academy might congratulate themselves at having been party to this happy cure. Now, let any one of you who is not satisfied just say so and I'll see to it that he is hanged!"

Thereupon the learned men and bigwigs turned tail and went off in the same order that they had come, frightened at this threat, and squinting at their noses to see if their faces were not even longer still.

But the king, after having dismissed these gentlemen, called Punch and spoke about the value of travel as a means of completing his education. Punch saw that it would be well for him to be out of the way, and was delighted, for he had long realized that his proper place was not among these stupid people, and that the court of Naples was a cramped setting for his activities. Moreover he was so well advanced in his studies that his teachers could find nothing more to teach him; he had even made scientific discoveries of which they were ignorant. In short, like all people of liberal cast, Punch found himself drawn toward France as his natural home. He therefore quickly agreed with the king that a trip would be a good thing, and it was arranged that he would set off the next day without fail.

The news of Punch's departure was not a secret for long. It brought comfort to the heart of Lord Boogoo-Roogoo and to the breasts of the academicians. In fact the whole court, save the princess, felt relieved to know that its dull mind would be delivered from fear of his keen one.

But the common people of Naples felt otherwise about Punch's impending exile. "He's leaving! He's leaving!" they wailed in the squares, in the streets, from door to door, from window to window, and from dormer to dormer. "Our own Punch! The sworn enemy of that wicked Boogoo-Roogoo! The friend of the people, he's leaving! Shed a tear, good folks! Drink his health! Ah me, we'll be losing our dear hunchback forever! Let's drown our sorrow in a cask of wine, let's drink all night! Let's dance! Music, ah me, music!"

Thus cried the people of Naples, half laughing and half weeping like the sun in a shower. Lord Boogoo-Roogoo was entrusted with levying taxes, and loaded these poor people miserably with them. They had no better consolation than to laugh at those who made them suffer, and they had every reason to regret Punch's going.

Punch was tying up his little bundle of belongings and packing his books, guitar, and mathematical instruments when he was waited upon by a deputation of market women and poor people of Naples. He received them simply, moved by

the honor they did him. After words of regret the speaker for the group wound up by saying, "It's a good thing that you're going, Punch, that you're free to go. Look at us, friend! We can't. We have children, or we are old; we're tied down here for life. We'll have to go on living under the heel of Boogoo-Roogoo unless you can find some way of putting him out of favor with the king for good."

"I'll give some thought to it, comrades," said Punch, very much affected. Thereupon the deputation went off smiling at this assurance from the people's favorite.

Punch knew that the king would pardon his nobles anything but a breach of etiquette. Thus when Lord Boogoo-Roogoo had lately killed a man by beating him, the king had punished him with nothing more than a slap on the cheek, whereas the same day a courtier who had forgotten to doff his hat when the king passed by, in less time that it would have taken to fasten his garter, was seized and beheaded. It would therefore be necessary, if he were to lose favor, to cause Lord Boogoo-Roogoo to commit some blunder of form. Unfortunately there was no one better versed than he in etiquette, or more willing to be found dead than at fault in its observance. Though that was all he knew, he had it at his fingertips, as a fool may know a thing by rote.

Punch was not discouraged, however, from finding some way to make him slip. It would have to be some grave offense against court etiquette,

some breach of custom without precedent. Now
Lord Boogoo-Roogoo was in the habit of taking
snuff; every five minutes he had to have recourse
to his snuff-box. With this as his point of attack,
Punch spent the night mixing snuff with a pow-
dered plant he had discovered in his botanical
studies. It had the singular property of causing
the sniffles in any nose which ventured near; it
set off a series of explosive sneezes; it forced its
victim to use his handkerchief or die. Having completed the mixture, Punch put it in a snuff-box
exactly like Lord Boogoo-Roogoo's.

The next day, which was the eve of Punch's
departure, Lord Boogoo-Roogoo served as gentleman of the bedchamber. It was his duty, when
the king retired, to hand him his nightshirt, in
accordance with the form of those days.

Before Lord Ernest went up to the bedchamber
for this ceremony, the page who served him had
been at pains to remove the handkerchief and
snuff-box from his pockets, as Punch had asked
him to do. When the grand majordomo had
reached the royal presence he felt in his pocket
for his box, and not finding it, bade his page,
who was in the antechamber, to go back and
look for it. On the stairway he met Punch, who
gave him the box containing the mixture, with

the injunction not to hand it to his master until
the king was ready to put on his nightshirt.

The page suspected some trick but followed
his instructions. He waited in the antechamber,
watching the routine through the keyhole until
the king was out of his hose. Then he entered
puffing as if out of breath and handed the snuff-
box to the grand majordomo, who was now holding the royal nightshirt.

Lord Boogoo-Roogoo lost no time; he opened
the familiar box and took a pinch. The king's
day shirt had just been taken off. Feeling the
effects of Punch's powder, Lord Boogoo-Roogoo
gave a great sneeze, then was seized with an over-
powering desire to blow his nose. He searched
hastily for his handkerchief. He couldn't find it.
He couldn't hold back a minute, a second more.

He lost his head and blew—honk! honk!—right in the nightshirt he was holding.

"How's this?" boiled the king. "You! Ernest! Blowing your nose in the nightshirt of your sovereign!"

"Sire—" began the majordomo. But a new impulse seized him irresistibly—honk! achoo! honk! —and the shirt was blown out in such a bluster of sneezes that it seemed to be caught in the winds of battle.

"Ernest! Grand majordomo! Lord Boogoo-Roogoo!" stormed the king as he shivered between the two shirts, but the nobleman was deaf to protests, and not knowing what he was doing—whisk!—bundled up the nightshirt and stuffed it into his pocket.

"Let another nightshirt be brought us!" screamed the king. "And that idiot, that clown, that noxious nose-blower, that rude volcano—really, there's no other name for him—let him be put into chains!"

"Sire, sire—" the offender protested.

But now the king was deaf. "What scullery manners!" said he. "My shirts for dish-towels!"

But alas! An accident impossible to foresee now put Punch in a worse fix than the majordomo. The king—also addicted to snuff—mechanically happened to take a pinch, as he was gesticulating, from the fatal box that Lord Boogoo-Roogoo still held open in his hand. In his anger the king charged his nose as if he were ramming a cannon.

The explosion was terrific. Stunned by its force, and having at hand nothing but his day shirt, his majesty waived fine distinctions and gave it the same treatment that Lord Ernest had given his nightshirt.

This was sufficient to exonerate Lord Boogoo-Roogoo. Punch, who along with most of the palace, had run in upon hearing the noise, saw that all was up. He did not wish the blame to fall upon his comrade the page. "Sire," said he, "here's the culprit at your knees."

"Let him—achoo!—" commanded the king, "be —honk!—hanged this instant! Drive his parents from the palace and let his—achoo!—donkey be— honk!—drowned without due process of law!"

VI

How Punch Destroyed an Army of a Hundred Thousand Englishmen without an Ounce of Gunpowder—Punch Leaves Naples and Italy

THE KING ORDERED PUNCH'S EXECUTION TO TAKE place immediately by torchlight, for there could not be too much hurry in punishing temerity which had exposed the royal dignity to such an affront. Without loss of a minute the gallows was erected in the palace courtyard; the halberd guard was drawn round about in battle line; the crowd stood behind it, sad and quiet; and on the main balcony of the palace the king and Lord Boogoo-Roogoo awaited the enactment of the cruel spectacle.

The executioner placed the rope around poor

Punch's neck and started to mount the ladder. The king gave the signal and cried, "Ready!"

Just then a loud murmur broke out in the crowd and a horseman, covered with dust and bespattered with blood, broke through and came to a stop under the royal balcony.

"Sire," he shouted, "I bring news. Your army has been decimated by the English. Lord Hull à Ballou, heading a hundred thousand men, is marching on Naples. By tomorrow night he will be before your walls!"

The bearer of ill tidings had scarcely finished before the halberd guard, seized with panic, took to its heels in every direction.

"What am I to do?" lamented the king. "There's not a soldier left to defend us against the enemy. Who will save me and my people from the slaughter which certainly awaits us at the end of the day which I now see breaking?"

"I will," piped up Punch, "if you won't hang me any more."

At these words the crowd sent up a cry of joy and the king scrambled down from his balcony, ran to Punch, embraced him, and begged his pardon for having wanted to execute him. "Let everyone obey the orders of Punch this day," commanded His Majesty, "as if they were our own."

Again in possession of his liberty, Punch asked that every mirror in Naples be collected, round ones, square ones, even tiny pocket mirrors. Having learned the direction from which the English were approaching, he had all the mirrors carried out of town and hung along the walls facing that way. There were so many of them that they covered half a mile of ramparts from top to bottom, so thickly that there wasn't a chink as wide as your little finger. After these peculiar tactics Punch had hundreds of candles set out along the mirrored walls and the edge of the moat, which was wide and deep on that side, the candles so linked with fuses that they could all be lighted at once.

These preparations completed, Punch, with about thirty candle-lighters, took a position on the walls, watching out for the approach of the enemy.

At nightfall the formidable English army appeared in orderly formation over the hills. Expecting battle, it came to a halt to catch its breath. Lord Hull à Ballou, the English general, took his field-glass and surveyed the plain where he supposed Naples to lie. He looked to the right and he looked to the left but he saw nothing. It was too dark.

Punch, knowing by the sound that the enemy was near, had given the signal to his men. From the top of the walls, using long poles, they lighted the candles.

Seeing the burst of light, General Hull à Ballou shouted to his lieutenant, "Come here, Grapeshot. The enemy lights its beacons."

"Aye, sir," said Grapeshot, "I can make out the Neapolitan army."

It was, of course, their own soldiers, cavalry and infantry, which these two officers descried afar, reflected by the illumination of the candles in the mirrors hung on the walls.

"Damnation!" cursed Lord Hull à Ballou, using his glass again, "there's a lot of them! I can't understand why there isn't more noise out of so many troops. What order and discipline! But what's that? Why, their general is looking at me with his glass. The rascal does me the honor of wearing a uniform just like mine. Gad, but he's ugly looking!"

For, as you perceive, it was he himself that Lord Hull à Ballou mistook for the Neapolitan general.

"Let's have a look," said Lt. Grapeshot, taking his turn at the glass. "Why, you're wrong, sir. It's me that that rascally enemy general resembles!"

"No, it's me!" insisted Lord Hull à Ballou, taking back the glass and peering through it again.

"Pardon, sir," said Grapeshot, heating with anger, "it's me, I tell you!"

"You, you insulting knave?" barked the general, drawing his sword. And there's no telling what might have happened next if Punch and his thirty candle-lighters had not at that moment set up a fanfare of yells and trumpet calls.

" 'Tention! Take arms!" bawled the English general, forgetting his private quarrel. "The enemy attacks! To battle, men—on the double!"

They could see the army before them fall into ranks and start on the march toward them, all in the mirrors, to be sure.

"They approach!" bayed the general. "Look at them! Forward, forward! Sound your trumpets! Hup, hup! Faster, faster!"

Thereupon the English cavalry, with the infantry close behind it, hurled itself toward the town. The closer they drew to the ramparts, the clearer was the reflection in the mirrors and the closer the enemy seemed to be. Nearer and nearer they came, struck with terror by the nasty snarling faces which they thought to be those of the enemy. Nearer and nearer—they could almost touch the enemy—they raised their arms for the clash—then crash, bang! horses, horsemen, and foot soldiers piled up one on the other, somersaulted over the candles, and disappeared in the water of the moat.

A hundred thousand English perished. You can well imagine how the people of Naples acclaimed Punch when he came down from the ramparts.

"There he is!" they cheered, "our liberator, our savior! Brave and noble Punch! Our blessings on you forever!"

Now the king, seeing the triumph of Punch, found himself not without an ignoble feeling of jealousy. Coldly thanking him for his services, he shut himself up with Lord Boogoo-Roogoo and the two put their envious heads together to plot Punch's destruction on the morrow. They determined to put poison in one of his favorite delicacies, chocolate caramel creams.

As it fortunately happened, the princess overheard the plot through the partition. In all haste she betook herself on her light feet to the room of the page to whom she owed her life and told him everything. Heart-broken at this black ingratitude, Punch let a tear trickle down and drop on the hand of the good princess, who was not displeased at it. Then, taking only time enough to throw his arms around his parents and kiss his donkey on the ear, he had himself smuggled aboard a Spanish felucca and sailed for Marseilles.

VII

The Terrible Danger Faced by Punch on His Voyage—How He Escaped—His Encounter with a Turkish Pirate

THE CREW OF THE SPANISH FELUCCA HAD NO SUCH reasons as the people of Naples to hold Punch in respect. They did not fail to take note of his crooked form and joke about his two humps.

The captain had no idea of Punch's mettle, and was a poor humorist. He pointed to the hump on Punch's back and said, "Why not put down your baggage?"

Punch smiled and replied, "In this company it's safer with me."

"I presume that France is the right place for you. They take to handsome fellows there. Some princess is sure to fall in love with you."

"No, that's not why I'm going there. It's because I've heard that in France those who laugh at their neighbors' infirmities are held to be dolts." Thereupon Punch turned on his heel and went to his berth, leaving the captain abashed.

But the next morning when Punch climbed to the bridge to see the sunrise he ran into the captain again. He was shoved roughly aside. "Out of my way, there!" growled the captain. "You'll interfere with the navigation. Back to bed with you!"

"Sorry, sir. But rather than get in the way, I believe I can help. First, I think we're in for a storm by the looks of the horizon."

"That's a good one!" sneered the captain. "A landlubber teaching an old sea dog like me his trade!"

"Very well, then, drown if you must," said Punch and went back to his cabin.

The captain only laughed at Punch's prediction, and was joking with his sailors about the hunchback when the wind suddenly changed, the sky grew black, the sea rose, and the felucca started to dance like a marionette on the waves.

Punch came up on deck again and went to the captain. By this time the man was shaking with fear because of the storm. Those who bully the weak are the ones who shrink from danger. With the greatest coolness Punch said, "I told you that you'd be drowned."

The captain, who should have been busy getting his ship ready for the storm, flew into a fury. All he could think of was revenge upon Punch.

"You foul hunchback!" he yelled, "if I drown you'll go down before me! You must be some sort

of a sorcerer to have known of this storm. I've followed the sea for twenty-five years and saw no

signs of it. Men," he went on, speaking to his
frightened crew, "it's this hunchback, this sorcerer, who conjured up the storm! Throw him
overboard!"

"Overboard with him," echoed the crew. And
poor Punch was held over the rail, suspended between sky and sea.

In this desperate situation he did not lose his
head. "See here, fellows," he said, "it won't be
long before you join me with the fishes. Over there
comes something which will avenge me in a jiffy."

Everybody looked where Punch was pointing.
He was answered with a moan of terror. Scarcely
a quarter of a mile away gleamed the cannon of a
Turkish pirate ship, its sails full set, bearing down
on the felucca.

"Merciful heaven!" blubbered the captain,
"they'll run us all through with their scimitars
and marlinspikes!" He rolled on the bridge in an
agony of terror.

"Shipmates," said Punch, "a fine brave captain
you've got there! I might have saved you from the
clutches of the pirates, seeing that I have a smat-
tering of Turkish, but you were about to drown
me, I believe, before this interruption?"

Thereupon the crew went down on its knees
around Punch, begging him to forget bygones,

and not to abandon them, poor folks and fathers of families that they were, to the barbarity of the Turks. As for the captain, they bound him hand and foot, and begged Punch to command the vessel instead. Thus it is that knowledge and merit sooner or later find their place in the world and command their due.

Punch made only one request, that the captain be taken down into the hold so that his whimpering might not be heard. Then he went to his cabin and dressed himself as a Turk, which gave him an even more remarkable appearance. He let himself down into the ship's boat and rowed off with all speed toward the privateer, which was now hardly a hundred strokes from the felucca.

Now Punch had taken care to sprinkle his oriental costume with a nauseating herb juice, so strong

and repellent that it was painful to get even a
whiff of it. Thus perfumed, Punch came along-
side the Turkish ship and was hoisted aboard. At
the sight of the Turkish hunchback the pirates
were surprised; at the smell of him they recoiled,
holding their noses.

"Don't mind it," said Punch, and went to seek
the pasha who commanded the privateer.

"Salamalek, pasha," said Punch in his best
Turkish.

"By the prophet," muttered the pasha, "what a terrible odor!"

"Don't mind it," said Punch. "My good friend, I was taken prisoner by those villainous Spaniards. I hope you're going to seize their ship. Luckily I was able to escape and—"

"Pardon me, brother," interrupted the pasha, "but what is that devilish stench?"

"Don't mind it," said Punch. "As I was saying, luckily I escaped—"

"But you do stink most unconscionably!"

"Don't mind it," repeated Punch. "Since I escaped, I hope—"

"By my beard," cried the pasha, "just between us, young man, you've got something wrong with you."

"Don't mind it."

"Not mind it! I can't keep my mind off it! You poison the air."

"It's nothing," said Punch, "it's only the plague."

"The plague!" screamed the pasha, jumping up and doing his best to render his nose airtight. "Plague it!"

"Of course, sir, nothing but the plague. Really nothing at all. All the Spanish crew died of it, so you'll have no trouble taking the felucca."

"By the Hellespont!" burst out the pasha anew, "I'll take neither it nor you, you infected wretch! Get away! Quick! Have them push you off in your boat, you walking plague! Men, let's strain every sail to escape. The felucca is plague-ridden!"

While the pasha was still sputtering with panic, Punch got back to the felucca, where he was received with transports of joy. For the pirates could be seen turning tail (or sail) like the thieves that they were, and they were soon out of sight.

The rest of the voyage was very pleasant, and when Punch landed in Marseilles, the crew were sorry to part from him, for they had grown to know him for his goodness of heart as well as for his wit.

VIII

*Reappearance of the Soot-Black Cat—Punch's
Ride—What Happened to Him in the Forest*

Losing no time once he was off the ship, Punch
went to look for a horse on which to post to Paris;
he was impatient to get there. He had to look no
further than his inn. There he found a pretty
Arabian which seemed high-spirited and well able
to cover the ground. While he was in the inn yard
concluding the bargain with the host, a big soot-
black cat came and rubbed his legs, meowing
softly.

"Does this nice cat belong to you?" he asked
the host.

"That it does, sir," replied the host. Now this man's name was Cascaillou and he had a sly face.

"A handsome animal," remarked Punch.

"And the best of my postilions," said Cascaillou with a wink. He stood with his hands in his breeches pockets, jingling the money he had just received from Punch.

"You're a sharp one. What do you mean?"

"I mean just that. Why, this cat knows the road to Paris so well, he has it at the tip of his paws. I've let lots of travellers use him; he never fails to give satisfaction."

"Really? If that's so I'll take him," said Punch. "At least I'll have something to remember you by as a swindler."

He paid for the cat as well as the horse, mounted, and—whoosh!—away he went.

No sooner was he off than Cascaillou, rascal that he was, burst into laughter and sank to a bench by the door, holding his sides.

Punch rode lickety-split along the road to Paris. What surprised him was to see the big cat, its legs twinkling, keeping well ahead. "Certainly a remarkable creature," he thought. But his surprise changed to uneasiness when the cat went faster and faster, and the horse after it, as if they were blown by the very fury.

The horseman saw trees, houses, towns, steeples, and dumbfounded travellers whiz by to right and left like hazy images in a dream.

"Stop! Stop!" people called after him along the way, but before they could make a move, cat, horse, and rider were out of sight.

"It must have been the devil," said townsfolk. "It was something, anyway, to get a glimpse of him."

"Hey!" gasped Punch. "See here, cat! Look, old boy! Aren't we going to stop somewhere for dinner? What's the rush? Aren't you feeling a little too exuberant? Whoa! Gosh! My breeches are burning up!"

But nothing seemed to dampen the ardor of the cat, and Punch hurtled along hour after hour, panting to catch his breath.

Now listen to what happened. At nightfall the big cat, the horse, and Punch were sailing through a somber chestnut forest, still at the same speed, when suddenly all three plunged into the earth and disappeared like magic.

IX

What Punch Tumbled into, and How in a Spirit of Fun He Skewered a Robber Band

IN THE CHESTNUT FOREST WHERE PUNCH WAS SWAL-lowed up there was a trap door which pivoted on its center. No sooner did anything step on one end than it was pitched head first into the earth.

Punch and his horse came tumbling down, feet in air, into the middle of some thirty characters of very rough appearance. Not only were their plumed hats pulled down almost to their moustaches, but their huge boots were pulled up almost to their waists. They had expressions to match and an arsenal of arms. And the whole company was lighted by dozens of flickering torches.

"Hello, everybody," said Punch, getting his head at the proper end and nodding to this amiable assemblage.

"Welcome, Punch," replied the robbers with a roar of laughter—for they were certainly robbers. The one who seemed to be their leader came forward. He was Captain Snortle; a black patch covered one eye and almost half his face; his nose— but we'll come back to that.

"Our band is in need of an inventive brain," said Captain Snortle, "a brain such as yours. We know you by reputation. That's why I sent my big grayish cat, which has something of the sorcerer about it, and Cascaillou, a member of our society, to Marseilles to bring you here without delay. I hope that you'll stay and be one of us, for if you refuse, I've no alternative but to boil you alive in our stew-pot."

"Knowing myself as I do," said Punch, "I'd

rather not be boiled alive. Gentlemen, I am therefore yours, body and mind."

"If that's the case, give me your hand," said Snortle. "Now follow us."

The robbers filed out of the little chamber under the trap door and started down an underground passageway which sloped so steeply that Punch had difficulty keeping on his feet. This descent was well over five hundred feet long. At the bottom, led by Captain Snortle, Punch entered a succession of caves where the sun never penetrated. They were lighted day and night by lamps hung from the rocky vault. There it was that this gang of miscreants dwelt, carousing over the ill-gotten spoil of their expeditions.

Punch saw that despite his friendly reception a close watch was kept on him. There was little

chance for him to escape with a whole skin by any ordinary means. He spent the night turning over in his mind a plan of escape which was remarkably bold and dangerous. But he was willing to risk violent death in order to get out of this infernal hideaway.

That very night Captain Snortle chose ten men and went off with them on a job. Our hero knew that there was nothing to gain by waiting. The time was ripe for his daring attempt.

The next day when they awoke, the robbers, Punch in their midst, took their places in the dining cave around the table, planted their elbows on it like the boors they were, and set to gobbling. When he saw that the feast began to pall, Punch spoke up.

"Comrades," said he with a satisfied grin, "it's a charming life that you lead here. But I confess that this delectable feed leaves me with only one regret. I miss the entertainment which we used to have at the court of Naples after meals. It settled the food and helped digestion."

"Yes? What was that?" asked the gang.

"I mean the roller coaster. You glide down a slope, as you know, going faster and faster, in little cars all in a line, with grooves or tracks to guide their wheels. It looks to me as if you have the ideal place for a roller coaster here, in the passageway along which we came last night."

"Grand idea! Just the thing! What a brain this hunchback has!" cried the robbers all together. They got up with a single desire. "Fellows, let's set to work. Punch, show us how to build a roller coaster. We went to have one right away."

So these rogues found axes, saws, and hammers,

and set to work putting wheels on packing boxes for cars and laying rails down the passageway. Punch scurried here and there, giving directions and supervising the construction, urging them on with words of encouragement, and giving a little hop of joy or rubbing his hands when he was unobserved.

Soon everything was ready. They drew the twenty cars—every bandit wanted one for his very own—to the top of the slope in the chamber under the trap door, and arranged them in a train on the rails. It took only a little push to start them down. At Punch's suggestion, to give the roller coaster a festive brilliance, the vault and walls of the tunnel were covered from top to bottom with such numbers of torches and candles that it looked like the staircase in a fairy palace.

Punch himself asked no more than to stay at the bottom and watch the fun. To this they made no objection. He was to give the starting signal by three claps of his hands.

Clap, clap, clap!

The twenty cars, each with its robber, start down the slope. They gain headway. They plunge along with fearful speed.

What's that in Punch's hands? They are half way down. From behind his back Punch has drawn a kitchen spit more than thirty feet long,

adequate for the mighty robber feasts. He fixes it
with its point on a level with the onrushing cars.
They see it and howl. Too late! Zip, and it goes
through all twenty. A terrible death, but a fit
punishment for their crimes.

Punch did not sit down and wait for Snortle to
return. He dragged the skewer with its amazing
birds to a wagon which he found in the underground stables, hitched six horses to it, and took
the first beaten trail which he found in the forest.
In less than two hours he reached the city of
Chartres.

X

Punch Finds a Surprise in Chartres

AT THE RUMBLE OF PUNCH'S WAGON OVER THE cobblestones, the citizens of Chartres peered out of their windows. At the sight of the strange little parade—twenty skewered bandits raised like a banner—down they came into the street, young and old. After Punch they thronged—tramp,

tramp, tramp—to the square in the center of town, today called the Place des Épars.

It took but a minute or two for Punch to explain his adventure. When he had finished, those who had come to jeer at his appearance stayed to shake his hand and kiss his garments. For these very thieves that Punch had exterminated had been preying on the city night after night. They had stolen bells from the belfries, cannon from the arsenals, and even policemen from the police station, right under the nose of the commissioner.

To escape the enthusiastic crowd, Punch asked the way to the commissioner so that he could make his report, deliver his evidence, and finish the matter without further delay. But the crowd was not easily shaken off. They unhitched the horses and dragged their liberator's wagon themselves.

When Punch entered the little room where the commissioner was awaiting him, he was thunderstruck at what he saw. That nose! It was unmistakable. He had last seen it sprouting from the countenance of Captain Snortle. It was no common, garden variety of nose, easily forgotten after it was seen, but a wonderful tropical plant of a nose. It appeared ten minutes before its owner. It protruded like the bolt from a cross-bow, the cannon from a carriage, or the shaft from a wagon. Its tip was enhanced with a wart surmounted by three red hairs, waving aloft like a plume.

No two such noses could exist under the sun; Punch could not be mistaken. Though the commissioner was without the patch which Snortle had worn over his eye, Punch perceived that he must make an audacious combination of the functions of law and larceny. No wonder he had not been able to apprehend himself!

But Punch pretended not to recognise Snortle in his official uniform, and Snortle pretended to be delighted to see him. He pressed our hero to tell of his escape, and while he listened, stroked a big cat that purred beside him. Then he praised Punch for his courage and invited him to supper.

XI

*How Punch Landed in Prison—The Devil's Tail—
A hitherto Unknown Method of Escape*

OUT OF THE CORNER OF HIS EYE PUNCH SAW THE
table set with a wonderful-smelling ragout, steam-
ing hot, a home-made pie, and three cobwebby
bottles. "Commissioner, do you really want me to
stay for supper?"

There is no use pretending; it must come out
sooner or later. Punch, as you may suspect, had a

liking for sweets. And he liked all the pleasures of the table. He was as fond of eating as of good deeds. Thus you see that the invitation to supper with the commissioner, a supper which promised rare good cheer, was a great temptation to him, especially as he was very hungry after his exertions.

"Then I'll be glad to join you," said Punch to the bogus commissioner, forgetting prudence and sitting down at the table between Snortle and the black cat.

Just what happened at supper is not very clear. Punch afterwards confessed that he himself couldn't quite remember. Some think it might have been the ragout, some the bottles. But he passed out, we are sorry to tell.

This much is certain. When he woke up the next morning, he found himself on a bed of straw in a damp place, with only a trickle of daylight coming through the bars. It took no great reflection to know that he was in jail, and that the bogus commissioner had put him there to be rid of a witness to his crimes. He thereupon wondered if he might ever again see the outside world. His head in his hands, he bethought him of the pleasant cottage in the orange grove where his parents lived, of the affectionate farewells they had given each other, and of the mournful look of his donkey as he had taken his last leave of him. These memories brought tears to his eyes.

"Who's that I hear crying?" suddenly said a voice near Punch.

Punch sighed. "A fisherman's poor son, with a hump at his front and his back, and a pretty low opinion of fame."

"What makes you say that?"

"It's like this," explained Punch, heaving another sigh. "I wanted to rise above my humble birth by my knowledge and cleverness. A palace door was open to me; I had my fill of splendor; but that's all it meant. I found only hatred and injustice. But who are you? You don't seem any more fortunate."

"They call me Peter Patience. I'm a puppet showman. I entertain the poor and the children. Some day the world is going to be a better place, but until then I make people laugh at its abuses. That's why I fell afoul of the commissioner."

"Why, of all the—!"

But Punch was rudely interrupted. The door of the dungeon swung open on its rusty hinges and the commissioner stepped quickly in, followed by his big black cat. In the glimmer of a torch held by the jailor, the livid Snortle read the sentence of the two prisoners. They were condemned to hang within an hour for having been part of the bandit gang in the forest!

Punch was about to protest against this flagrant injustice, but the commissioner sneered and turned on his heel. The big cat was following its master. Punch was furious. He gave the door such a slam behind them that the animal's tail was caught and cut straight off. Instantly it changed into a squirming rope, lashing itself into a tangle. At the end was a yellowish tuft which gave off a strong smell of brimstone. Here is a picture of it:

Warranted a true facsimile. B.

"Look what we have," said Punch, holding up the remarkable tail. "What do you think, Peter Patience? Should we wait until they come and take us to the gallows?"

"No," said the puppeteer, "but what else can we do?"

"Look," proposed Punch. "I'm pretty sure that this tail is the devil's if it isn't his grandmother's. I read somewhere in an old book that the devil never travels on any steed but his tail. All he has to do is to say where he wants to go, and he's there in three shakes."

"Let's try it," said Peter Patience. "We'll have to get the best of the devil with his own instrument.

That ought to be permissible for good people. Anyway, we have no other choice."

So Punch straddled the rope, holding the tuft as a bridle, and the puppeteer got on behind him.

"All set?" asked Punch. "Good. Now we'll try. Giddap! Paris!"

Just then the commissioner rushed in, followed by the executioner. He stood petrified on the threshold. The two prisoners disappeared up the chimney, and the three red hairs on the end of his nose turned white.

XII

AND LAST

*Punch in the Champs Élysées—Why this Story,
Truthful to the End, Has no End*

PUNCH HAD SCARCELY HAD TIME TO SEE WHERE HE
was going before he found his feet on the ground
in the beautiful Champs Élysées, with Peter Patience beside him. It was a marvelous spring day,

and the smiling promenade was lively at this mid-day hour with the happy prattle of children, the songs of street singers, and the cries of sidewalk entertainers. Paris seemed to be the most agreeable place of entertainment in the world.

"What a happy place! I'd love to spend the rest of my life here!" exclaimed Punch. "No kings, no grand majordomos, and no police commissioners!"

"What's to prevent you?" asked the puppeteer, winking.

"I haven't a penny in my pockets, my baggage was left behind in Chartres, and I'd rather eat a little too much than too little."

"Listen, I've got an idea!" said Peter Patience. "I'll set up my puppet booth here. It can't fail to be a success if you'll consent to be an actor in it. Your wit and your odd appearance (begging your pardon) will surely draw the crowds."

"I believe you're right. Among the great I found nothing but envy and spite. To what better use could I put my natural endowments than to amuse the poor and the children, always so simple and good? I'm poor myself, and my place is humble. My job is to make them laugh! To see their beaming faces will be my reward. I'll do it!"

"Shake hands on it, then," said the puppeteer. "Tomorrow you'll make your debut."

"Wait! One condition! One of your puppets must be a police commissioner so that I can whack him to my heart's content in memory of that fellow in Chartres."

"Wonderful! I was going to suggest it myself."

So Punch made his debut the next day. What an effect he made on the public when they saw him for the first time, with his grotesque costume, his variegated humps, his impossible chin, his sharp, compelling voice, and his dexterous play with the longstaff! But they went wild with enthusiasm when the surly commissioner entered and this dialogue ensued:

COMMISSIONER. What's your name?

PUNCH. Same as my father's.

COMMISSIONER. And your father's?

PUNCH. Same as mine.

COMMISSIONER. None of your insolence! Will you tell me your name?

PUNCH, *showing his stick*. If you'll tell me what this is.

COMMISSIONER. It's a stick.

PUNCH, *whacking him*. A stick? It's a flute!

COMMISSIONER. Ouch, ouch! All right, it's a flute.

PUNCH, *whacking him*. A flute? What's the matter with you? Can't you see it's a bugle?

Commissioner. Ouch, ouch! Help! Mercy! Yes, it's a bugle!

Punch, *whacking him.* A bugle! Trying to be funny with me, are you? It's a piano.

Commissioner. Ouch, ouch! Yes, a piano!

Punch, *raining whacks.* Silly, silly man! It's a stick. *To the audience:* That's the way to do it! That's the way to be sure you're right!

In short, Punch was so well content with the good will shown him by the public and with his pleasant engagement in the Champs Élysées, after all his gruelling adventures, that he stayed there for years, as fresh and young as ever whenever he played. But every evening when his shows were over he used to get on the devil's tail, which he preserved carefully, and whisk off to Naples to bid his parents good night.

On one of these nocturnal visits he took it into his head to remind the good people of Naples of his existence, and to have one more joke at the expense of the high and mighty who had treated him so badly. So he went to one of the most crowded theatres in Naples wearing a mask, and appeared on the stage between acts. They thought that one of the actors of the regular troupe had donned the celebrated costume to play a comic scene, never guessing that it could be Punch himself. But the reception they gave him was no less warm for that. However, he had scarcely made his first point when there was such an outburst that he was almost snowed under with flowers.

The next day the sallies of the mysterious actor were going from mouth to mouth all over town, to the discomfort of the courtiers and academicians against whom they were directed. Spurred on by this success, Punch made it his custom to appear in this way to the people of Naples every night, to amuse them at the expense of their common foes. For this reason he still enjoys tremendous popularity in Italy even today.

Nevertheless he remained faithful to the country of his adoption because of the delightful way of life it had given him. Only once did he fail to return to Father Peter at his regular time, and then he was absent from the puppet theatre in the Champs Élysées for a full fortnight. The children of Paris were bitterly disappointed. "Where has he gone?" they asked.

"To Naples, I presume."
"What's he doing? Why does he stay away?"

On this point we can only hazard a guess, Punch having always kept the deepest silence about this dark period of his life. When he returned it could be seen that his wonted gaiety was tempered at times with a shade of melancholy; a wrinkle, caused perhaps by some emotional blow, changed the usual serenity of his brow; he would sometimes wipe away a tear which intruded into his slapstick routine. Punch had grown from carefree youth to manhood through the sorrow which comes to all.

Thenceforward he got Father Peter to add a new puppet to the company, a woman who might share some of the whacks so bountifully showered on the commissioner. This fancy was all the more surprising in Punch, who was never lacking in gallantry. There seems to be no explanation for this callousness save that he was disappointed in love.

A learned Neapolitan told me, and I have no reason to doubt his word, that Punch was detained for the fortnight in Naples by an affair of the heart. Columbine, the daughter of old Pantaloon, was the object of his affections. But neither Punch's serenades nor his sighs had the slightest effect on her. And at last he was brought to see with his own eyes that she had a preference for

Pierrot, because of his interesting pallor, which changed in a moment to one for Harlequin, because of his healthy color. But why should he have fallen in love with such a flutterbrain of a girl? I confess it's beyond me.

This is all that I am able to tell of Punch's story. As it continues every day in the open air for everyone who attends his theatre, it would be presumptuous to go further with what is none of my business. Go hear it the first fine day that you can. You'll be sure to meet me there.

OCTAVE FEUILLET

FOR THOSE WHO WANT TO KNOW MORE ABOUT THIS STORY

OCTAVE FEUILLET'S FATHER, A BRILLIANT AND DIF-
ficult man, could not have done better to start his
son on a literary career. He forbade him to write,
urged him to enter the diplomatic service, and cut
off his allowance. Octave was honor-bound to become a successful writer. So he settled down in
Paris to scribble novels under the pen-name of
Désiré Hazard (a young writer need hardly say
that he is courting risk) and to concoct plays.
His one-act fantasy, *Le bourgeois de Rome*, was
produced at the Odéon with no particular recog-
nition on 15 November 1845, and a five-act drama,
Échec et mat, was performed at the same theatre
on 23 May 1846 because it was a vehicle for his
collaborator's uncle who acted there.

So far, not so good! Though Octave could de-
pend on his brother Eugène, two years older than
he, who was also in Paris, dutifully working in the
ministry of finance as his father wished, to treat
him to dinner now and again, the landlady had to
be paid, and he welcomed any writing assignment

that came his way with a few ready francs. Such must have been the story for young readers, *Vie de Polichinelle et ses nombreuses aventures*, which appeared with the imprint of J. Hetzel, 76 Rue Richelieu, in 1846, when he was twenty-five. (Octave was born at St Lô, 2 Rue St. Georges, second floor front, on 11 August 1821 at 3 P.M.— they are precise about these matters in Normandy!)

In the story there is not a little of the liberal enthusiasm which he probably received from his father's family, with a dash of the disenchantment ("Among the great I found only envy and spite") which might belong to a struggling young hack as well as to Punch. The picture of a perfidious king must have been a little embarrassing years later when Feuillet, now famous and well off, accepted the post of palace librarian at Fontainebleau under Napoleon III, and was honored to have the Empress Eugénie act in an amateur production of his play, *Portraits de la marquise*. It must be said against the budding novelist, however, that when he made Punch ask for a female puppet for the express purpose of beating her, it is hard to explain his bitterness toward the fair sex; at least he had not yet married Valérie Dubois, the cousin who made him so good a wife.

It may have been the charm of Punch's life and adventures—a charm which has made them classic —which accounted for their frequent reprintings, and it may also have been Feuillet's growing fame which stimulated interest in anything that he signed. There were French editions in 1860, 1879, and probably many before and after which were undated. An English translation, *The Life and Adventures of Punchinello*, appeared so early as 1852 under the imprint of D. Appleton & Company in New York, to be reprinted in 1856, 1857, and perhaps later. A new translation by Marian Ford was issued by G. Munro in New York in 1881. These are typical Victorian translations, and their euphemisms and omissions form a catalogue of the inhibitions of the era.

An Italian translation, *Vita di Pulcinella*, by Luigi Lazzarini, came out in the Edizioni Aurora, Milano, 1936. The episodes of the story are recognisable in *Punch's Merry Pranks, a Little Play for Little People*, published about 1850 with fifteen hand-colored woodcut illustrations, by William Tegg and A. & S. Joseph, Myers & Company of London, and printed by Friedrich Volck-mar of Leipzig. A complete bibliography of the book might prove both interesting and formidable.

The present translator has tried to make a readable version by being as colloquial as the original, and by bringing a little knowledge of puppetry to bear on his wording. He confesses that, because of the phobias of 1946, he has suppressed a phrase and sometimes a whole sentence where Feuillet grew too sentimental or moralistic!

Mention of Bertall the illustrator must not be omitted. His real name was Charles Albert d'Arnould (1820–1882) and his span was close to that of Feuillet (1821–1890). A deft and prolific draughtsman, he produced as lengthy a list of titles as did his collaborator on the life of Punch. At least once he was an author, when he collected and illustrated *Les contes de ma mère* in 1877.

Lives of such Italian masked-comedy characters as Punch have tempted many a whimsical pen. *La chronique des marionnettes*, a 1765 pamphlet (translated in *Puppetry 1937*, pp. 55–56), is an account of Punch in which the names of real puppeteers and players appear. From such quasi-history Feuillet may have got his idea. But the presence of Punch himself in the Champs Élysées, not yet crowded off the miniature boards by the upstart Guignol, would have furnished sufficient data. The year is not far wrong when Punch's birth is fixed at the time of the storyteller's grandfather's great-uncle's visit to Italy. It was indeed near Naples, around the year 1600, that the mask of Punch came into being. Soon afterwards it was preëmpted by a puppet; the puppet reached Paris by the mid-seventeenth century. This is as long a story as Feuillet's. I've told it in greater detail in my introduction to the Limited Editions Club's handsome *Punch and Judy*.

I am tempted to trace the influence of these adventures of Punch in other books. Did the pranks —fishhooks to snatch wigs, for instance—lead Wilhelm Busch into creating the deplorable *Max und Moritz* (1865), who must be held responsible for innumerable naughty boys, including the Katzenjammer Kids? Did the adventures have something to do with Pinocchio, who first saw the light of day in 1880? There seems to be not only a kinship of mischief but a family resemblance.

His story of Punch was only a starting point in Feuillet's career. From it he went on to such bestselling novels as *Bellah, La petite comtesse*, the tremendously popular *Roman d'un jeune homme pauvre*, and what is probably his masterpiece, *M. de Camors*. He composed many successful plays, starting with *La crise*. In all this careful and urbane writing there is nothing, however, more enduring in delight for the reader than the exploits of Punch, which he may have dashed off to pay for a month's lodging.

The portrait of Punch on the jacket of this edition of his adventures is redrawn from a color lithograph by W. Sharp which appeared on the music for the *Quadrille de Punch*, published by William H. Oakes and for sale by John Ashton & Company, 137 Washington Street, Boston, Massachusetts, about 1850. It was printed by Bouvé and Sharp, also of Boston. This portrait appeared on music both in England and America, and one engraved version of it emanated from Sydney, Australia. As a companion piece there was a portrait of his helpmate on the *Valse de Judy*, a color lithograph by Bufford printed by B. W. Thayer & Company of Boston shortly afterwards. This couple looks far more British than French or Italian; Judy is, of course, a native Englishwoman.

PAUL McPHARLIN

FOR THOSE WHO WISH A PUPPET THEATRE OF THEIR OWN

IT IS FUN TO READ ABOUT PUNCH'S ADVENTURES, but even more fun to see them on the stage. You can build your own little puppet theatre and act them out, amusing your friends and family in your living room. The work of construction can be as pleasant as the performance.

A puppet Punch can be made and operated in several ways. When Punch appeared on the Champs Élysées in Paris his theatre was a booth about the size of a shelter for the signalman at a railroad crossing, and Punch was a hollow bag over the puppeteer's arm, with his head and hands stuck on the puppeteer's thumb and first two fingers. The action took place within a frame over the puppeteer's head; he held his arm straight up so that only the puppets over his hands could be seen.

But there are simpler kinds of puppets. You can make flat ones from cardboard. Copy the Punch on the cover of this book. Give him separate arms and legs pivoted with the kind of paper fasteners that have two shanks to bend over flat, or with string knotted tight on each side with knots bigger than the holes through which the string passes. Support the whole figure with a piece of heavier cardboard or a flat stick, painted black and glued to the back of the body. A wire to one of Punch's hands will control his gestures. The other arm and legs can be moved by the swinging of the supporting stick. Punch can now appear over the back of a chair or within a little stage over your head. He will dance to music, or you can make him tell about one of his adventures. Then you can make the king of Naples, Lord Boogoo-Roogoo, Captain Snortle, and other characters the same way, and face them toward Punch for dialogue.

As the next step you can make round figures, but of cloth instead of cardboard. Cut cloth patterns for bodies and limbs, two for each part, allowing about half an inch extra for the material taken up by the seam, sew them together, stuff them with cotton or scraps, and attach a supporting stick and hand rod. (Old umbrella ribs are very good for hand rods.) These round puppets can be costumed as elaborately as you wish, so long as their joints can move.

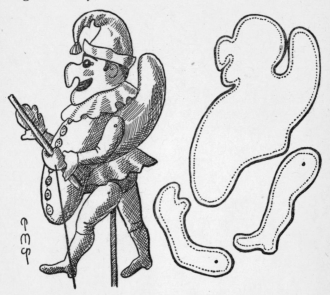

A hand-puppet Punch can be made with a stuffed cloth head and hands, and a body like a shirt just big enough to fit over your hand and cut to its shape. This sort of puppet is much easier to make than a full jointed figure worked with strings from above, but it is possibly more difficult to operate until you develop a lot of finger dexterity and the ability to hold your arm over your head without tiring. It is easy to make a

hand-puppet dance or bang another over the head with a stick, but much harder to make it do quiet acting. Watch that the puppet doesn't keep sinking out of sight below the stage opening—and never, never let your arm be seen where the puppet bag stops! It's worse than a slip showing.

If you know something about whittling or modeling, you can carve Punch's head and hands of wood; sometimes he even has legs sewed to the front of his body, and these can also be of

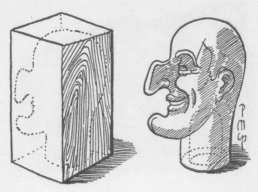

wood. Or you can model the parts of clay, take plaster molds, and cast them in papier-mâché or wood pulp. But this process takes considerable skill. Paint the finished head with oil colors well thinned with turpentine; oil-paint drier or linseed oil as a thinner gives too much of a shine, as if Punch were feverish (which he may sometimes be!).

Good lights on your area of action are more important than scenery. A curtain or flat surface will serve as a background, but you must have plenty of light on the puppets themselves, not on the background or shining into the eyes of your audience. A bridge-lamp or two with shades that can be tilted to control the spill of light may be placed at the sides of your stage. Christmas-tree lights as footlights are amusing but not very practical. If you want to develop your stage further,

you can make special miniature spot- and border-lights, a switchboard with dimmers, a proscenium frame (keep its decoration in scale with the puppets), a velvet front curtain, and as much special scenery as you please. But all this takes a lot of time, and sometimes gets in the way of the play—the play's the thing.

These hints are merely to show you what you can do. They are far too brief to help you in all the problems you will encounter if you turn puppet showman like Peter Patience. (When you have solved these problems you'll know why Punch's puppeteer friend was given that name.) You will need to read some of the books which have been prepared to help puppet showmen. Here are a few of them that your book shop can order, or your public library may have on its shelves:

Marionettes, Masks and Shadows, by W. H. Mills
and L. M. Dunn. 1927.

Be a Puppet Showman, by Remo Bufano. 1933.

A Manual of Puppetry, by R. Bruce Inverarity.
1938.

How to Produce Puppet Plays, by S. Hastings and
D. Ruthenburg. 1940.

There are many puppet plays ready written for
your use, and you'll find over a hundred listed in
this pamphlet:

A Producer's Guide to Plays for Puppets, by Paul
McPharlin. 1932.

There are even histories of puppet theatres:

A Book of Marionettes, by H. H. Joseph. 1920.

Adventures of a Russian Puppet Theatre, by Nina
Efimova. 1935.

Puppets in America 1739 to Today, by Paul Mc-
Pharlin. 1936.

And when you become an ardent puppeteer
you may join the Puppeteers of America, the
national society of American puppeteers, and receive its yearbook, *Puppetry*, and its news-letter,
The Grapevine Telegraph.

P. McP.

D.C. PUBLIC LIBRARY

3 1172 02117 0816